Fatuma's New Cloth

By Leslie Bulion

Illustrated by Nicole Tadgell

Moon Mountain
PUBLISHING

North Kingstown, Rhode Island

First edition.

Cataloging-in-Publication Data (updated from Library of Congress Data)

Bulion, Leslie, 1958-
    Fatuma's new cloth / by Leslie Bulion ; illustrated by Nicole Tadgell.
      p. cm.
    Summary: In East Africa, a young girl learns that one cannot always judge
by appearances as she and her mother visit a market in search of kanga cloth
and meet merchants who all claim they have the secret to good chai (tea).
    ISBN 0-9677929-7-5 (hardcover) (alk. paper)
    ISBN 1-931659-05-2 (paperback) (alk. paper)
    [1. Conduct of life—Fiction. 2. Markets—Fiction. 3. Africa, East—
Fiction.] I. Tadgell, Nicole, 1969- ill. II. Title.

PZ7.B911155 Fat 2002
[E]—dc21
                                                    2001044832

Moon Mountain books are available in bulk and with customization for
promotional use. Contact the publisher for details.

Moon Mountain Publishing
80 Peachtree Road
North Kingstown, RI 02852
www.moonmountainpub.com

The illustrations in this book were done with Winsor & Newton Artist's
Watercolors on Arches 140 lb. hot press bright white paper.

Printed in South Korea

10 9 8 7 6 5 4 3 2

In memory of *marehemu* Jamal.

And for Sue, with love and boundless gratitude.
L.B.

For my wonderful, wonderful Mother;
and in memory of Sam-Sam.
N.S.T.

"I am glad to have your help in the market today, Fatuma."
"I like to carry the basket for you, Mama."

"At the cloth shop, you can choose a new kanga cloth. We will sew you a dress."

"But I want to wrap my kanga like you."

"You are small now. When you are bigger you will wrap your kanga like me."

"Mama, I am big! I already help you sew.
Soon I will go to school and learn to read. Will
you read me the words on your kanga, Mama?"

"Let's see. My kanga says: *A small daughter named
Fatuma is a blessing.*"

"Oh, Mama!"

"Yes, I am teasing. My kanga says: *Your family is
your blessing.*"

"Will we sew my new kanga when we get home from the market?"

"Yes, Fatuma. And I will make us chai to drink."

"I love chai just the way you make it, Mama. What makes it taste so good?"

"My tea leaves make perfect chai," said the man who sold tea and spices. "You can see the chai is good by the dark color. Here, have a cup."

"That chai looks very dark and strong, but it does not taste sweet like yours, Mama."

"Of course not!" said the woman who sold milk. "Chai is good only when it has a light color—the color it gets from my creamy milk. Come in my shop and taste!"

"That chai is very creamy and light, but
it does not taste sweet like yours, Mama."

The pot seller laughed. The pots and pans on his cart shook and jangled. "Who cares what you put in the chai if you don't make it in the right pot? Try the chai in this shiny new saucepan."

"The chai does look beautiful in that shiny new saucepan, but it does not taste sweet like yours, Mama."

"Here we are at the kanga shop, Fatuma.
What color kanga cloth do you want?"

"I want a kanga the color of the deep sea
and the early morning sky."

"I am sure I have something that will please you," said the kanga seller. "What about this one?"

"That kanga is nice, but it is the color of eggplant and new grass."

"Don't worry! I have many others. Hmm . . . how about this one?"

"That one is very pretty too, but it is the color of tomatoes and the sky at midnight."

"Oh, I think I know just what you want, my child. Not this one . . . not this one . . . but wait . . . what do you think of this one?"

"Oh yes, that kanga is just right—the color of the morning sky meeting the waves of the sea! What are the words on my kanga, Mama?"

"Your kanga says: *Don't be fooled by the color. The good flavor of chai comes from the sugar.*"

"But Mama! When I look at chai, I can see the dark color of the tea leaves. I can see the creamy milk. I can see the shiny pot. But I can not see the good flavor from the sugar. It is inside!"

"Just so, my little Tuma. Now let's look at you. If I look at your hand, will I see that you are my helper in the market? If I look here behind your elbow, will I see how hard you work at your sewing? And where can I look to find all of your good questions?"

"Oh Mama! You can't see those things at all. What is good about me is on the inside, too!"

AUTHOR'S NOTE

Women in East Africa wear bright cotton kanga cloth over their dresses to keep them clean of dust and cooking stains. A woman might wrap one kanga around the waist of a dress and another over her shoulders, or head and shoulders. A small girl like Fatuma can wear a play dress made from one kanga folded in half with a neck hole cut in the middle. Kangas are also used as baby slings.

Each kanga pattern is printed with a Swahili saying. Many of the sayings have more than one meaning. The kanga that inspired this story was printed with the saying, *"Usihadaike na rangi tamu ya chai sukari."* In English this means, "Don't be fooled by the color. The good flavor of tea is the sugar." It also means that you can't tell whether people are good by looking at them. When people say, "Don't judge a book by its cover," they mean the same thing.

Chai is the Swahili word for tea. East African chai is often cooked with milk and is quite sweet. Tea masala, or tea spices, can be added for more flavor.

Here is a recipe for East African chai:

    2 cups of water
    2 cups of milk
    3 teaspoons of loose tea
    2 teaspoons of sugar
    2 cardamom pods
    1/2 teaspoon of vanilla
    1/4 teaspoon of ground ginger

Boil all ingredients in a medium saucepan for five minutes. Strain into a teapot. Serve with additional sugar and milk to taste.